SATI
the Rastifarian
By Edgar White

illustrated by
Dindga McCannon

Lothrop, Lee & Shepard Company   New York

SATI

Sati was of the mountains. Of the West Indies. His eyes were two black circles in a sky of white. His legs were long twigs. His skin was night black. Oil from the coconut made his hair soft.

Sati had lived five years of days and nights. The days he had watched by the sea. The nights carried voices.

Sati could run the day long among the always upward trees. There were many secrets to be learned. First, there were the secrets of the fruits. The mango said if you bite into me you will find a sweetness like heaven. And then the warmth running out. Next was the secret of the sugar cane. If you eat me you will suddenly become strong and very happy. Then there was the secret of the sea. Every fish gave a different taste and a different wonder. Even the raw saltfish gave pleasure.

One evening before Sati fell asleep, he remembered his mother
say, "Soon you will have to leave us and go very far away to

the place they call America." Sati did not think much more about this. He was not sure that what he heard was real.

Then it was a Monday. Sati was sure that it was a Monday because the day before had been Sunday. On Sunday he had been taken to the sea where he saw his cousin baptized in the waters. It was at this place that Sati himself had been baptized. It was not in the same water, however, because the old water had flowed out and come back new.

Yes, it was a Monday, and a tall woman with a red dress and a hat with a feather arrived. She was his aunt, they told him. Aunt Marie from the place that was America. She had come to take Sati back with her. Her hands were open and she smelled of perfume, leather, and cars. She stayed for several days in Sati's house, which was high on a mountain near the sun.

Aunt Marie said, "You will like it very much in America."

"No, I do not think so," said Sati, as politely as he could.

Aunt Marie smiled a smile of two dimples. Then she said, "In America you will get an education. You will learn from the masters, the wise men."

"Who are these men?" asked Sati.

"They are called teachers and professors," said Aunt Marie.

Sati knew that he did not want to leave, but one day they led him to the sea. The water made the sound of groaning as it beat the sides of the ship they took him on. The ship was called *The Deinos.*

"I want to go back home. I want to go back home so bad," cried Sati. And the whistle of the ship blew, and black smoke rose above his head.

Aboard the ship, Sati met a tall sailor who was from Sati's island. The sailor was born in the mountains of the West Indies and they called him a *Rastifarian*. He looked into Sati's eyes and saw tears.

"Why are you crying, little *Rastifarian*?" asked the sailor.

"Because they are taking me away to the place they call America," said Sati.

"And you do not want to go?"

"No," answered Sati.

Then the sailor lifted Sati and looked deep into his eyes. "Because you must go to a place far away from the colors of your home, I will give you the gift of memory and of dreams," he said. "No matter how far you go, they will go with you."

And Sati stopped his crying. Beneath them the dark sea moved like a black fan, and the blue of the sky lay down upon them.

They arrived in New York City and from the pier Sati saw buildings taller than he had ever seen before. He heard more noise than he had ever heard before. For the first time in his life Sati felt the cold, and he found that they called this winter.

His aunt stopped a car named TAXI, and they got in. They drove all around the city and Sati looked out the window at the millions of other cars. There were men standing in the middle of streets blowing whistles so loudly they turned red in the face. There were many lights flashing. Everyone looked as if they were running. So this was New York!

"I do not think I will like this place," said Sati.

Aunt Marie just looked at him and smiled.

Then the taxi arrived uptown where the poor people lived. Sati could tell that this was where the poor people lived because it was darker here than downtown and the expressions on the faces were different. Everyone looked surprised, as if they did not believe this was how they lived. The people did not speak much but just looked from their eyes.

"This is where we live," said Aunt Marie, and her glasses slid to the tip of her nose.

Time passed and Sati was sent to school. His teacher's name was Miss Gold. She spelled her name for the class and then wrote it in large letters on the blackboard: GOLD.

The first week of school Aunt Marie showed Sati the way. After that, he was on his own. Almost every day he was in a fight with someone. Usually it was the older boys who were used to beating up smaller boys. Sati did not like people to bother him. But secretly . . . he loved to fight.

One day Aunt Marie took Sati to a doctor for an examination. The doctor listened to Sati's heart through a long rubber tube. He placed one end on Sati's chest and placed the other two parts in his own ear so that he could listen. Then the doctor said, "Okay," and Sati smiled.

The doctor looked in Sati's mouth and throat. Again he said, "Okay," and again Sati smiled.

He looked into Sati's eyes with a little flashlight. Then he had Sati read the letters on an eyechart far across the room. Sati tried, but he could not see the letters clearly. This time, the doctor did not say, "Okay." Sati had to start wearing glasses. Now he got into more fights than ever before.

In the spring of the year Sati discovered the park. He met friends his own age there by the swings and slides, and beneath the trees. Before Sati made friends, he used to talk to the trees. He would tell them about the trees in the West Indies. Then the trees would blush green.

Then he met Omar, Selah, and Dija.

Dija's mother was a painter. She was very poor but she could make beautiful paintings and the people in her paintings were in love with each other. Sati wished he had beautiful colors above him on the wall when he slept the way Dija did.

Selah's mother was a dancer and her father played music on a large bass. When Selah's mother wanted to dance Selah's father would play for her. Sometimes when Selah danced she would look like her mother. Her father was so tall that people had to step back to see all of him.

Then there was Omar. His mother was the best cook in the universe so they always liked to go to Omar's house.

Sometimes Sati would tell his friends about his own country. He would tell how he had seen a hurricane and lightning that destroyed a tree with a flash of fire. Or, Sati would tell about carnival times, when the people dressed up in their dreams.

How there were no electric lights and the people carried lamps at night. How once he had seen some men on stilts taller than even Selah's father. The others listened to Sati and their eyes grew big.

It was in July when the sun tried to sneak its way into New York City that Sati wrote a letter to his mother:

my dear Mother,
. I miss you very much. America is very far from where we live. It is not so cold now as when I first came. Now it is very hot like at home but there is no wind from God.
I wear glass on my eyes now. I do not like it but it is O.K. You have told me to stay here. I will stay here then. I obey aunt Marie. I have friends here now. Omar and Selah and Dija.
Last week was Aunt Marie's birthday. I gave Aunt Marie some flowers then she cried on me and kiss me.
I miss our house.
I miss you.
well good bye. Love you,
Sati
P.S. I will come back on the sea To see you.